"Goodnight Pitt Panthers"

By Samantha Hawthorne

ISBN: 979-8-6657-1766-1

Goodnight

Pitt Panthers

There's a school that's known for excellence.

It's better than all the rest.

Panthers never falter.

Pitt Panthers are the best!

Panthers love to win,
they never lose it.

It's an honor and a privilege,
to be a Pittsburgh student.

They study to be doctors and lawyers,

musicians, and dancers.

They study hard for exams,

to learn all the answers.

But now, it's getting late.

It's time to say goodnight.

Goodnight, beautiful campus.

Goodnight, incoming freshmen.

Goodnight, Heinz Field.

Goodnight, student section.

Goodnight, homework.

Goodnight, tests.

Goodnight, Pittsburgh...

you are the best!

Goodnight, Mom. Goodnight, Dad.

One day, I too...

will be a Pittsburgh grad.

Goodnight, Pitt Panthers!

Made in the USA
Middletown, DE
21 December 2024

67994149R00015